THE LAZ DUCK

WRITTEN AND ILLUSTRATED BY: JAYSON D. ZOLLER

The Laziest Duck is written and illustrated
by Jayson Zoller
Copyright 2004, Jayson Zoller

Published and Printed by:
  Lifevest Publishing
  8174 S. Holly Street #107
  Centennial, CO 80122
  www.lifevestpublishing.com

Printed in the United States of America

I.S.B.N. 1-932338-52-7

THE LAZIEST

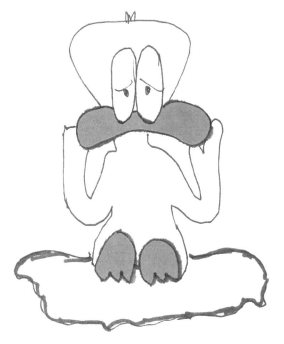

DUCK

In a little duck kingdom in a far away land,
There was born the Laziest Duck.
He was much too lazy to play with his friends,
So he sat all alone on a rock.

The other ducks would ask him to play,
But always he'd say in his lazy duck way,
"Not today. Not today,
I'm too tired to play!"

He continued sitting alone in the sun,
While his friends were playing and having great fun.
He would not swim. He would not run.

4

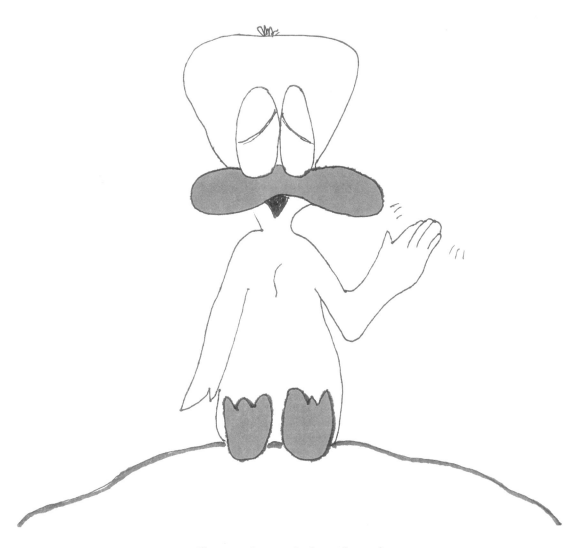

He was happy being the only one
Who would sit and say in his lazy duck way,
"Not today. Not today,
I'm too tired to play!"

Then one afternoon, he began to get hungry,
As all little ducks sometimes do.
To his surprise, he realized
That he could not move to get food.

Being lazy had made him round and fat!
He couldn't get up without help
And THAT was THAT!

He began to be sad,
That he always did say,
"Not today. Not today,
I'm too tired to play!"

He cried out for help
In a series of quacks,
And his friends came running
From this way and that
To see what had happened
To the duck who just sat.

9

They couldn't help laughing
When they saw on the floor,
The fat little duck
Who couldn't get up anymore.

He said if they'd help him,
He'd never be found
Being lazy again
Just sitting on the ground

So they pulled him off
of his grassy mound
And the once lazy duck
Began dancing around.

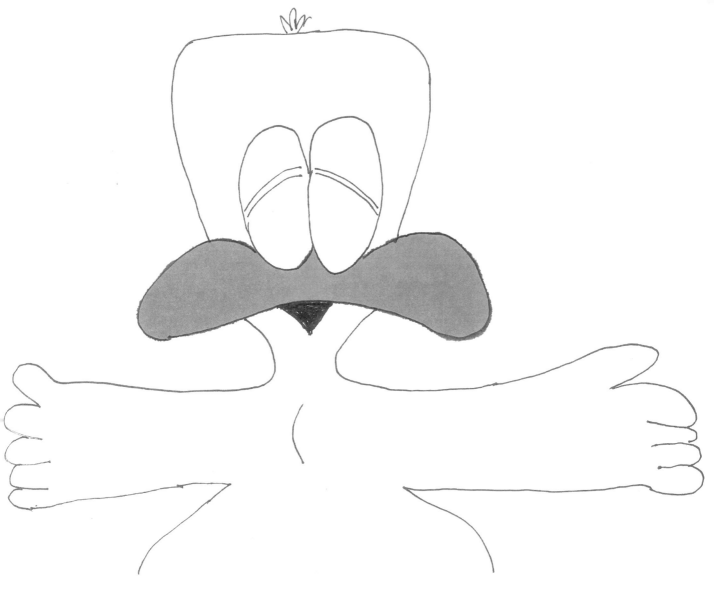

From that day on, he played and he played.
And he liked to say in his new kind of way,
"Today, today, today, is the day,
Please come my way, I WANT TO PLAY!"

To Order Copies of

THE LAZIEST DUCK

ISBN 1-932338-52-7

You may order online at:
www.authorstobelievein.com

by phone at:
877-843-1007

by mail:
Just send check or money order to:
**Lifevest Publishing
8174 S. Holly Street #107
Centennial, CO 80122**